The Witch Who Wanted to Be a Princess

Lois G. Grambling ❧ illustrated by Judy Love

◖◗ Charlesbridge

To my handsome princes—Ty, Mark, Jeff, and Art—
and to my beautiful princesses—Lara and Marcia
— L. G. G.

To Alexandra, who selflessly toils to transform this *witch into a princess,*
and a special thank-you to my own Frank and Bella—Darrell and Pamela
—J. L.

2007 First paperback edition
Text copyright © 2002 by Lois G. Grambling
Illustrations copyright © 2002 by Judy Love

Published by Charlesbridge
85 Main Street, Watertown, MA 02472
(617) 926-0329
www.charlesbridge.com

Library of Congress Cataloging-in-Publication Data
Grambling, Lois G.
The witch who wanted to be a princess / Lois G. Grambling; illustrated by Judy Love.
p.   cm.
Summary: When a Grand Wizard puts a ban on witches changing themselves to
princesses, Bella must marry a real prince to make her dream come true.
ISBN 978-1-58089-062-5 (reinforced for library use)
ISBN 978-1-58089-063-2 (softcover)
[1. Fairy tales.] I. Title.
PZ8.G7464 Wi 2001
[E]—dc21   2001004378

Printed in Korea
(hc) 10 9 8 7 6 5 4 3 2 1
(sc) 10 9 8 7 6 5 4 3 2 1

Illustrations done in transparent dyes on Strathmore paper
Display type and text type set in Quaint and Esprit
Color separations made by Sung In Printing, South Korea
Printed and bound by Sung In Printing, South Korea
Production supervision by Brian G. Walker
Designed by Diane M. Earley

Bella was a witch. But Bella didn't want to be a witch. She wanted to be a princess, live in a big castle, and wear silk gowns, dainty glass slippers, and a jeweled crown.

But Bella was a witch. She lived in a small cobwebby cottage, and wore a long black cape and big pointy shoes and a tall hat that didn't have any jewels on it.

You would think a witch
who graduated at the top of her class
from the School for Witches would be
able to change herself into something plain
and simple, like a princess. But Bella couldn't.

She could change bats into rats, and rats into
cats (that's how she got her favorite cat, Nightmare),
but Bella couldn't change herself into a princess.

Every time she tried,
her wand went limp, or
sputtered. Once it even
started to hiccup.

Bella was puzzled. She checked her copy of *1,001
Fail-Safe Spells and Enchantments* to make certain
she hadn't forgotten anything.

She hadn't.

So she consulted her computer. (Few witches used a crystal ball anymore.)

After searching, Bella's computer flashed this message:

Due to sharply declining numbers, witches have been declared an endangered species by the grand wizard. No witch (not even you, Bella) is allowed to change herself into anything!

Especially a princess. That's final! Have a nice day. :)

"Drat! And buckets of newts' eyes!" Bella said. "Now the only way for me to become a princess is to marry a prince. Not an icky one, of course, but a handsome one.

I hope we haven't changed
them all into frogs!"

They hadn't.

There were still a few left.
After weeks of scanning the
personal ads in the Sunday
newspaper, Bella found one
that sounded promising:

Bella read the ad again.

"No problem with the good family background," she said—her great grandfather had been grand wizard.

And her grandmother had been the first ever woman witch doctor.

"But that 'beautiful damsel' part could present a little problem," she said.

Bella thought the big wart on the end of her nose made her more beautiful than she already was. But Bella realized a handsome prince might think otherwise. And she was prepared, if need be, to remove it with a dab of *Potent Potion #13 Wart Remover*. But before doing something that drastic, she decided to check with her magic mirror.

Bella murmured, "Magic Mirror, look at me. Do you a beautiful damsel see?"

"Beauty is in the eye of the beholder, Mistress," it said.

Bella nodded. "I agree," she said, gazing with admiration at her reflection. "And since I, through my eyes, see myself as beautiful, that is how I am. *Beautiful!* The wart stays! And I'm glad. I've grown quite attached to it. Thank you, Magic Mirror."

"You are most welcome, O wise mistress," the magic mirror said.

Pleased and confident, Bella climbed onto her jet-powered broomstick and took off for the Kingdom of Styne.

Heavy air traffic and strong head winds delayed Bella's arrival.
When she landed on the castle roof, it was already after 3:00.

She raced down the stairs.

"Drat! And beakers of beetle juice! I hope I'm not too late!" she said, pushing past the many servants busily bustling about.

She was.

The throne room door was closed and locked. No matter how hard she pulled, she couldn't get it open.

Bella was beside herself. She didn't know what to do, until she saw the keyhole. She peeked through it.

The handsome prince was interviewing the last of the beautiful damsels. She wasn't too late if she could get in. But how?

Then Bella saw the open window. She clicked her big pointy shoes together three times and a small rocket popped out of each heel. Bella murmured, "Blast off. Quickly. Do as I say. To that window. Right away."

Unfortunately, when Bella reached the open window she was going so fast she slipped. And fell. And went tumbling head over heels to the floor below, landing *flop kerplop* in a heap at the handsome prince's feet!

"How clever to enter through the window, beautiful damsel. I am Prince Franklyn of Styne," the handsome prince said, bowing low.

"And I am Witch Bella," Bella said, pleased the handsome prince saw her as both clever and beautiful.

As Prince Franklyn helped Bella up . . .
their eyes met.

Sparks flew.

Lightning flashed.

It was love at first sight!

Prince Franklyn couldn't take his eyes off Bella.
He knew they were made for each other. He got
down on one knee and asked her to marry him.

Bella couldn't take her eyes off Prince Franklyn.
She knew they were made for each other.

"I will marry you," Bella said, giving
Prince Franklyn her hand.

Everyone in the kingdom was invited to the wedding.
And they all came. The food was free, and there was
lots of it. So the castle's main throne room was packed.
But Prince Franklyn and Princess Bella didn't notice.
They only had eyes for each other.

"You are so beautiful, my beautiful princess!"
said Prince Franklyn, gazing at his new bride.
"You are so handsome, my handsome prince!"
said Princess Bella, gazing at her new husband.

And that is the story of how Bella, the witch, became a princess.